LIBBY WIMBLEY

COW GIRL

Fountaindale Public Library
Bolingbrook, IL
(630) 759-2102

by Amy Cobb illustrated by Alexandria Neonakis

Calico Kid

An Imprint of Magic Wagon
abdobooks.com

For Kaylee and Fred~Thank you! –AC

To John, Kitty and Gooby for their constant love and support.–AN

abdobooks.com

Published by Magic Wagon, a division of ABDO, PO Box 398166, Minneapolis, Minnesota 55439. Copyright © 2019 by Abdo Consulting Group, Inc. International copyrights reserved in all countries. No part of this book may be reproduced in any form without written permission from the publisher. Calico Kid™ is a trademark and logo of Magic Wagon.

Printed in the United States of America, North Mankato, Minnesota.
102018
012019

Written by Amy Cobb
Illustrated by Alexandria Neonakis
Edited by Tamara L. Britton
Art Directed by Laura Mitchell

Library of Congress Control Number: 2018931806

Publisher's Cataloging-in-Publication Data

Names: Cobb, Amy, author. | Neonakis, Alexandria, illustrator.
Title: Cow girl / by Amy Cobb; illustrated by Alexandria Neonakis.
Description: Minneapolis, Minnesota : Magic Wagon, 2019. | Series: Libby Wimbley set 2
Summary: The county fair is coming up! Libby wants to enter a contest. She decides to show Fred the cow. When Fred acts up in the show ring, it appears all is lost. But Libby and Fred work together and learn first place isn't the only winner.
Identifiers: ISBN 9781532132537 (lib.bdg.) | ISBN 9781532132735 (ebook) | ISBN 9781532132834 (Read-to-me ebook)
Subjects: LCSH: Cows--Juvenile fiction. | Cowgirls--Juvenile fiction. | Farm life--Juvenile fiction. | Friendship--Juvenile fiction.
Classification: DDC [FIC]--dc23

Table of Contents

Chapter #1
A Fair Idea

It was a warm summer day. Libby Wimbley and her best friend, Becca, took turns on the tire swing that hung from the giant oak tree in Libby's backyard.

"It's almost time for the county fair," Becca said, giving Libby a push.

The fair! Libby loved the rides. And the yummy foods. And the fair's fun contests. Then Libby remembered something.

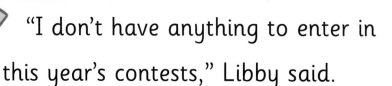

"I don't have anything to enter in this year's contests," Libby said.

"Seriously?" Becca sounded surprised.

"So what's your entry, Becca?" Libby asked.

"My top-secret banana bread recipe." Becca smiled.

That gave Libby an idea. She came back down to Earth then.

"I know!" Libby said. "I'll make a cobbler for the baking contest. Want to help me pick blackberries?"

"Sure!" Becca said.

The girls raced off to the blackberry patch.

Chapter 2

In a Jam

But when Libby and Becca got to the berry patch, there weren't any plump, juicy blackberries ready to pick.

"These are all red," Libby said. "The berries have to be black to make a blackberry cobbler."

Now Libby was really in a jam. What could she enter in the fair instead?

"Maybe you can knit a hat," Becca suggested.

Libby shook her head. "I tried knitting mittens once. But the thumb holes were upside down."

Both girls laughed about Libby's mixed-up mittens.

Then Becca looked toward the garden. "You can enter a prize pumpkin."

"Good idea," Libby said. "But the pumpkins won't turn from green to orange until fall."

Libby couldn't wait that long. The fair was next week!

Stewart, Libby's little brother, came by. He twirled a rope. Then he tossed it over a fence post.

"What are you doing, Stewart?" Libby asked.

"Practicing for the fair's roping contest," Stewart said.

Libby sighed. Even Stewart was doing something at the fair. And he was pretty good at it, too.

Chapter #3
No Fair

Libby and Becca headed to the barn next. It was Libby's favorite place on the whole farm. That's because all of the animals lived there. The animals—Libby had another idea!

"Becca, I've got it!" Libby said. "I'll show one of the animals at the fair."

"That's perfect!" Becca agreed.

But now, Libby had a new problem. Which animal should she enter?

"Otis, would you like to be in the fair?" Libby asked the pony first.

He munched on some hay. Otis was too busy to be a show pony.

Next, Libby asked the goat. "Elvis, how about you?"

"Meh-meh," Elvis said. Then he headed off to find shade under a tree. Elvis was busy, too.

"Want to go to the fair, Doodle?" Libby asked the rooster.

Doodle fluttered away. None of the animals wanted to be in the fair with Libby.

"Maybe I'll skip the fair this year,"
Libby sighed.

She leaned against the gate.

Someone nudged Libby's shoulder.

Chapter #4
Team Fred

"MOO!"

"Fred!" Libby laughed. "You silly calf."

He nudged Libby again. Fred wanted her to pet him. Libby did. So did Becca.

"Hey, Fred can be in the fair with me!" Libby said.

Becca gave Libby a high five.

"Why didn't I think of that before?" Libby wondered.

Mom and Dad came into the barn.

"Think of what?" Dad asked.

"Showing Fred at the fair," Libby said.

"Showing an animal takes a lot of effort," Mom said.

"I can do it," Libby promised. She looked at Fred. "I mean, Fred and I can do it!"

Becca smiled. "You'll make a great team."

"Team Fred!" Libby smiled, too.

Libby got right to work. Every day, she brushed Fred's coat and cleaned his hooves. Then she clipped a rope to Fred's halter. Libby led Fred around and around the pasture.

On the night before the fair, Libby
said, "Good job, Fred! I'll see you
bright and early in the morning."

Chapter #5

Scaredy Calf

The next morning, Libby met Fred at the barn gate with a sudsy bucket of water. She scrubbed Fred's coat until it shined.

"We're all ready for the fair, Fred," Libby said.

Mom and Dad helped Libby load Fred into the trailer. And they were on their way!

After a while, Stewart said, "There's the Ferris wheel!"

Libby couldn't wait to ride it. And she couldn't wait to show Fred.

Before the judging started, Libby brushed Fred one more time.

"You're moooo-ti-ful, Fred!" Libby joked.

Soon, the judging began. Fred pranced around the show ring with Libby, just like they'd practiced at home.

Suddenly, the crowd scared Fred. He lowered his head and kicked up his heels.

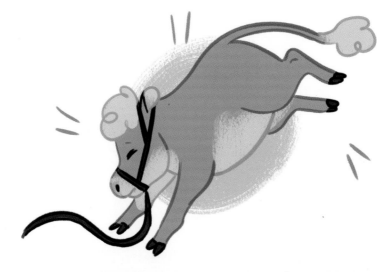

"Stop, Fred!" Libby shouted.

Fred didn't stop. He bucked up and down. This way and that.

Libby stayed calm. She tugged on Fred's rope. When Fred stood still, she patted him. "See, it's okay."

Libby and Fred finally finished their circle around the ring.

After the show was over, a judge said, "Now we'll award the winners."

"Go, Libby!" Stewart cheered.

The first place ribbon was given
out. Then second place. And third.

"Looks like we didn't win. But you
did great!" Libby smiled at Fred.

Then the judge announced, "And
fourth place goes to Libby Wimbley
and Fred!"

Libby was given a pink ribbon.
Mom and Dad ran over.

"Congratulations, Libby!" Mom said.

"You were a good sport, cow girl," Dad said.

"Thanks!" Libby smiled. Then she hugged her calf. "We did it, Fred."

"MOO!" said Fred.